P9-BZS-061

I Can't Stop!

A Story about Tourette Syndrome

Holly L. Niner

illustrated by Meryl Treatner

ALBERT WHITMAN & COMPANY, MORTON GROVE, ILLINOIS

To Brandon and Angie—Thank you for sharing
your struggles and triumphs.—H.L.N.

This book is dedicated to the memory of my parents,
David and Florence Treatner, for their
endless love and support.—M.T.

Library of Congress Cataloging-in-Publication Data

Niner, Holly L.
I can't stop! : a story about Tourette syndrome / by Holly L. Niner ; illustrated by Meryl Treatner.
p. cm.
Summary: A boy is diagnosed with Tourette syndrome and learns about constructive ways he can
manage his condition. Includes nonfiction information from a physician.
ISBN 0-8075-3620-2 (hardcover)
[1. Tourette syndrome—Fiction.] I. Title: I can not stop!. II. Treatner, Meryl, ill. III. Title.
PZ7.N62Iac 2005   [Fic]—dc22   2005003891

The design is by Carol Gildar.

For more information about Albert Whitman & Company,
please visit our web site at www.albertwhitman.com.

Note to Parents and Teachers

Tics are common; about 20 percent of children have them at some time. Usually they show up only as mild repetitive behaviors such as eye-blinking or throat-clearing. Most people think of these as "habits." Sometimes tics are worse. In as many as one in a hundred children, multiple motor (movement) tics and phonic (sound) tics come and go for years. Assuming the affected child is otherwise healthy, this is Tourette syndrome (TS).

Tics occur as frequent twitches or jerks, or slower, seemingly purposeful movements or sounds. Since the tics may vary over hours, days, or weeks, they may seem voluntary. The child may be labeled "nervous," and told to settle down. (Coprolalia, or compulsive cursing, can occur in Tourette syndrome, but it is uncommon.) Most people with TS have several tics over many years, and many affected people share similar tics. This points to a shared difference in brain wiring and chemistry.

Tourette syndrome is mostly a genetic disorder, but the genes responsible remain unknown. Research has shown a change in the size and function of cell groups deep within the brain. Brain cells communicate via chemical messengers (neurotransmitters), and there are abnormal levels of some neurotransmitters in the brain of a person with TS. The resulting abnormal communication within the brain causes the symptoms of Tourette syndrome. However, no blood test or brain scan diagnoses TS.

Obsessive thoughts, compulsive actions, and other anxiety symptoms may also occur in affected people. Children with Tourette syndrome may have ADHD symptoms.

Not everyone with TS has all of these symptoms. People with mild symptoms may never see a doctor for them. Tics wax and wane in childhood, but usually improve some in young adulthood, especially in women.

There is no cure for TS. Nor is there one best medicine for all of the symptoms. Medications control tics, but not all tics need to be treated, and not all medicines work for each person. Educating family, teachers, and peers about TS accomplishes much. One of the best sources for educational materials is the Tourette Syndrome Association website: http://www.tsa-usa.org.

Misconceptions and prejudice about Tourette syndrome are giving way to understanding and acceptance. It is a neurologic disorder, like migraines, seizures, or autism. Tourette syndrome does not stop most affected people from having the jobs, relationships, and lives that they want.

Laurence Walsh, M.D.
Assistant Professor of Clinical Neurology
 and Medical and Molecular Genetics
Director, Child Neurology,
Indiana University School of Medicine

"Stop winking at me," Nathan said.

"But you were winking at *me*," his sister retorted.

"Nathan, you've been doing that all week," Dad said in his you'd-better-stop-young-man voice.

Nathan squeezed his eyes shut, but when they opened, his lids fluttered like butterfly wings.

Mom and Dad looked at each other. "I'll take you to the eye doctor," Mom said to Nathan. "We'll find out what's wrong."

By the time Nathan saw the eye doctor, the blinking had stopped, but now he was sniffing. The doctor thought it might be allergies.

The next day Nathan's class was taking a test. The room was quiet except for Nathan's sniffing.

"Mrs. Mackenzie," Amy said, "I can't think with Nathan sniffing."

"Try blowing your nose," Mrs. Mackenzie suggested, handing Nathan a tissue.

"Thanks." Nathan was embarrassed. He blew his nose, but the sniffing only got worse. Nathan didn't want to sniff, but he couldn't stop.

In a couple of weeks, the sniffing stopped, too. Nathan was happy. A few days later, he was in the cafeteria with his best friend, Josh.

"What are you doing with your head?" Josh asked. Nathan saw that some kids were staring at him and laughing.

Nathan realized his head was snapping down as if his ear wanted to touch his shoulder. He couldn't help it. He tried to hide what was happening by bending his head to the other side. "Just stretching my neck," he said.

"Well, stop," Josh said. "It gives me the creeps."

Nathan tried to stop moving his head because the snapping hurt. But stopping made him feel restless. He felt his head jerk once more. The restless feeling went away, but now people were looking at him again. He felt scared. *Why won't my body listen to me?*

After school Nathan's mom drove him to a swim meet.

"Think we can win today?" Nathan asked Josh.

Josh was mad. "How can we, with your head jerking?"

"I *want* to stop." Nathan slammed his locker. "But I can't!"

During the race Nathan just thought about swimming. His head only moved when he wanted to breathe, like it was supposed to. And his relay team won the race.

As they left the pool, Mom said, "Stop doing that."

"I can't."

"That's not true." Mom sounded annoyed. "You didn't do it during your race."

Nathan felt the tears spill over. He didn't want to be different. His parents were mad at him. The kids laughed at him. Even Josh didn't understand.

"Don't you get it, Mom?" Nathan clenched his fists. "My body won't listen to me!"

"Don't worry." His mom patted his shoulder. "We'll figure this out."

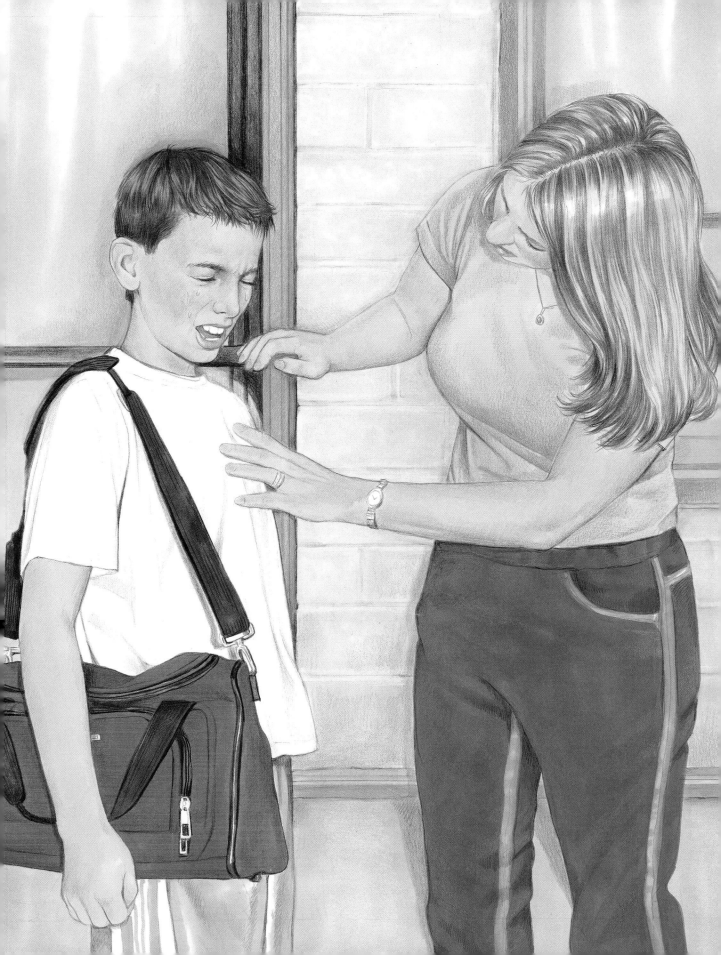

Nathan's parents took him to a special doctor. They told Dr. Phillips about the blinking, the sniffing, and the head-jerking.

"Those are tics," said Dr. Phillips. "Sometimes you feel like you have to do them, and other times you don't even know you're having a tic." He smiled at Nathan. "Lots of kids have them. If they continue for a long time, that's called Tourette syndrome, or TS. But sometimes they go away."

"I hope they do," said Nathan. "Sometimes they hurt. The kids make fun of me. And . . ." Nathan looked at his parents. "It makes my mom and dad mad."

"Nate, I'm sorry," said Dad, putting an arm around him. "We thought you were doing it on purpose."

"Especially," Mom added, "when you didn't jerk your head while you were swimming."

"Tics are like that," Dr. Phillips said. "When the brain is busy with other things, you might not have a tic. Sometimes you can hold one off, but it's like a mosquito bite. You can ignore it for a while, but eventually you *have* to scratch it."

"That's *just* what it feels like," Nathan said. "What makes it happen?"

"When you want to move any part of your body, one area of your brain sends a message to another," said Dr. Phillips. "Chemicals carry these messages.

"People with tics have too much of a chemical that turns movements on." Dr. Phillips took a can of marbles off the shelf. He took a marble out and dropped it in a cup. "Dropping the marble is like turning on a movement, but if I turn on too many . . ." Dr. Phillips dumped more marbles into the cup.

"They're spilling all over!" Nathan said as he picked the marbles up.

"That's how TS feels," Dr. Phillips said. "Too many movements are turned on, and you can't stop them."

"How can we help Nathan?" Mom asked.

"We'll see if the tics continue for a year. If they really bother Nathan, we can talk about using medicine." Dr. Phillips put the cup in a bowl and poured more marbles into it. Once the cup was full, marbles spilled into the bowl.

"But, like the bowl holds the marbles, there are things you can do to help control the tics."

Controlling the tics wouldn't be easy, especially when a new one could appear at any time. But Nathan hated the way the kids stared, so he and his parents looked for clues to manage the tics.

They made a chart to keep track of them. They found that if Nathan was tired, angry, or frustrated, the tics increased.

Nathan learned to recognize the restless feeling that came just before the tic. Then he could look for ways to block the tic or change it into a behavior people might not notice.

"Maybe," Nathan said, watching his arm move in the mirror one night, "when I feel an arm tic coming, I could put my hand in my pocket."

"That's a good idea." Mom wrote it down. "You could try fist-squeezing, too. That might release some of the tension, so you don't have to tic."

One Saturday Nathan and Josh went to the library.
"Do you think we'll get the project finished?" Josh asked.

"Sure," Nathan said. Then he surprised himself by barking.

"No dogs allowed," Josh said, smiling.

Nathan barked again. Josh frowned. "Nate, cut it out!"

"I heard a dog," said the librarian, coming by.

"No dog here," Nathan said, but as she walked away,
he barked.

She stopped. "You boys need to leave right now."

"I've had it!" Josh tossed his books in his backpack and
walked off. "You're always acting weird. I'm asking Mrs.
Mackenzie for a new partner."

Nathan hurried out the door after him. "Wait!" he called.
"I need to tell you something . . . I have Tourette syndrome."

Josh stopped and looked at Nathan. "What's that?"

"You should've told me sooner," Josh said after Nathan
explained. "I'm your best friend, aren't I?"

Nathan felt better. "The best," he said.

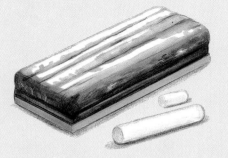

After Nathan told Josh about his TS, he and his mom told the class.

The kids had lots of questions. "I've heard of that," Eric said. "You can say bad words and get away with it." The class laughed.

"Most people with TS don't say bad words," Nathan's mom said, "but they like to show that kind of tic on TV."

"Lots of people have Tourette syndrome," Mrs. Mackenzie added. "They can still be anything. A doctor, ballplayer, even a teacher."

"First Nathan sniffed and then he jerked his head," Amy said. "Why did the tic change?"

"They don't know why the tics change," Nathan's mom said. "Or why the number of tics changes each day."

"Sometimes," Nathan said, "I don't even know I'm doing a new tic until it happens a lot."

"Will you always have TS?" asked Tyler.

Nathan looked at his mom.

She nodded. "Probably, but often people have fewer tics as they get older."

Each time Nathan's tics changed, he had to find new ways to handle them.

"I've started spitting," he told Josh, "so I'm searching for a way to change it."

"Could you swallow instead?" Josh asked.

"That might work." Nathan tried it.

Suddenly he spat. "Sorry about that. Changing tics takes practice."

"That's OK," Josh said. "I practice my spelling words every day, and I still get some wrong."

Nathan felt more relaxed now. At least his family and his class knew he didn't tic on purpose. He worked at controlling his tics, but sometimes things had to be changed at school or at home. When he started a tapping-his-pencil-on-the-desk tic, Mrs. Mackenzie put down a piece of foam so he could tap quietly. When he made *eh-eh-eh* sounds, his Dad wore headphones to watch TV. That way Nathan was free to tic, and they could still enjoy their favorite shows together.

Nathan tried to swim every day. When he swam, his energy went into the swimming, and there were no tics. All he thought about was slicing through the cool water.

There was a movie Nathan wanted to see, but going out with his family was hard. People might stare or laugh if he made strange sounds or his body twitched.

"We can sit on an aisle," Mom said, "so you can get up if you feel a tic starting."

At the movies Nathan held off his tics as long as he could, but finally he had to get up. As soon as he was in the hall, he started to twitch. An older boy saw him. "Hey, what are you doing?" he said.

Nathan had practiced with his parents. He had three choices.

He could ignore the boy and go into the bathroom.

He could say, "I don't do it on purpose. It's a tic."

Or . . .

He took a deep breath and said, "I have Tourette syndrome. It makes me move, and I can't stop it."

The big kid's face got red. "I'm sorry. I didn't know."

"Now you do." Nathan smiled going into the bathroom. *YES! I did it!*

One day on the way to the soccer field, Nathan and Josh saw some kids whispering and laughing. Josh was mad. "Those kids better stop," he said.

"This *is* a funny tic." Nathan laughed. "I call it "the chicken."

Josh smiled. "It *does* look like a chicken, but they shouldn't make fun of you."

"They don't bother me," Nathan said. "Not with a friend like you."

During the game Nathan took a shot and watched the ball fly into the net. As the kids cheered, he grinned.

He knew that the tics were part of him, but they wouldn't always get in the way. *Watch out, tics,* he thought. *You're not the only moves I can make!*